To my friend, Nick
—R.G.

Originally published in Great Britain 2005
By Little Tiger Press, An imprint of Magi Publications

This edition published in 2010 by Hallmark Books, a division
of Hallmark Cards, Inc., under license from Little Tiger Press.

Visit us on the Web at www.Hallmark.com.

ISBN: 978-1-59530-376-9
BOK1164
Printed and bound in China
JAN11

Clumsy Crab

by Ruth Galloway

LITTLE TIGER PRESS

Hallmark
GIFT BOOKS

Nipper the Crab hated his huge, clumsy claws. Snip, snap! Clip, clap! No matter how hard he tried, they always got in the way.

None of his friends had clumsy claws.
He wished he had tickly tentacles like Octopus
and Jellyfish or flippety fins like Turtle and the fish.

One day Nipper was playing catch-the-bubble with his friends.

They couldn't play that game any more. So they played tag instead.

Nipper scuttled off sideways, but one of his clumsy claws got in the way.

Nipper slipped and stumbled,
tripped and tumbled, until...

he was buried up to his eyes in sand. Turtle came to dig him out.

Everyone decided to play hide-and-seek.
Nipper climbed into a big clam shell and pulled
it shut.

It was the perfect
hiding place until…

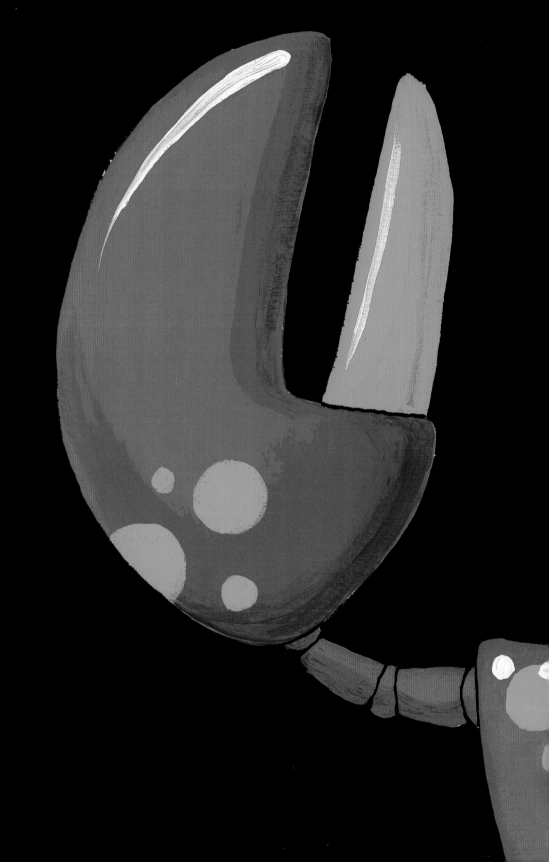

SMASH!

Nipper's clumsy claws shattered the shell into hundreds of tiny pieces. "Ouch!" he cried. "Help!"

Jellyfish picked up the pieces of shell.

"If I didn't have these clumsy claws, I wouldn't break everything, and I'd be good at hide-and-seek," said Nipper.

"Don't worry, Nipper," said the others. "We'll hide, and you can find us."

Nipper counted to ten, then set off to find his friends. He scuttled through the sand… and found Turtle.

He shuffled under the shells… and found Jellyfish.

And he searched up and down, in and out,
and all around the rocks...

but he couldn't find
Octopus anywhere.

Suddenly everyone heard a cry. Octopus was tangled up tightly in some seaweed!

"Help!"

Octopus squirmed and squiggled and wriggled and jiggled. Turtle and Jellyfish tried to help, but the knots just got tighter and tighter.

Nipper had an idea.

Nipper snipped at the seaweed with his claws. Faster and faster Nipper danced around the clump of seaweed, snipping and snapping, clipping and clapping.

His claws moved quickly, slashing and slicing, shredding and dicing, until the sea was filled with tiny pieces of swirling seaweed.

Octopus was finally free!

"Thank you Nipper! You're a clever crab!" he cheered.

Nipper waved his claws happily. At last he knew how useful they could be.